Hansel and Gretel

Illustrated by Eric Kincaid

SHOOTING STAR PRESS

Once there was a woodcutter. He was very poor. One day he said to his wife, "What will become of us? We are so poor we cannot feed the children."

His wife said, "We will take the children into the forest and leave them there. They must take care of themselves."

Hansel and Gretel
were listening at
the door. Gretel
began to cry.
"What will become
of us?" she said.
"Do not cry,"
said Hansel.
"I will look
after you."

When it was dark
Hansel went into
the garden. He
filled his pockets
with pebbles. Then
he went to bed.

Next day the woodcutter took the children into the forest. His wife gave them both a piece of bread. Hansel's pockets were full of pebbles. Gretel had to put the bread in her apron.

Hansel kept looking
back at the house.
"What are you
looking at?" asked
the woodcutter.
"I am looking at
my little cat,"
said Hansel. But
really he was
dropping pebbles
on the path.

When they were deep in the forest
the woodcutter made a fire.
"Sit and rest," he said to Hansel
and Gretel. "When we have cut the
wood we will come back for you."
Hansel and Gretel waited and waited.
Their father did not return.
At last they went to sleep.

When Hansel and
Gretel woke, it was
dark. They were
alone. Gretel began
to cry.
"Do not cry," said
Hansel. "As soon
as the moon rises,
I will take you
home."

The moonlight shone
on the pebbles
Hansel had dropped
on the path.
They followed them
all the way home.

Some days later Hansel and Gretel heard their stepmother plotting again. When she was asleep, Hansel went to fill his pockets with pebbles.

The door was locked. He could not get into the garden. Gretel began to cry. "Do not cry," said Hansel. "I will think of something."

Next morning their
stepmother gave
them both a piece
of bread. Hansel
put his bread into
his pocket.
He broke it
into crumbs.

"Why do you always
look back?" asked
the woodcutter.
"I am watching
my pigeon," said
Hansel. But really
he was dropping
crumbs along
the path.

The children were left as before.
The moon rose. Hansel looked for
the crumbs. They were not there.
Birds had eaten them. Now Hansel
and Gretel were lost.
Three days passed. Then they saw
a white bird. "It wants us
to follow it," said Hansel.

Hansel and Gretel followed the bird.
It led them to a house with walls
made of gingerbread. It had
a roof made of cake and windows
made of sugar.

Hansel and Gretel were hungry. They
broke off a piece of the house.
They began to eat.
"Nibble nibble like a mouse.
Who is nibbling at my house?"
said a voice. The children thought
it was the wind and took no notice.

The door of the house opened.
An old woman came out.

The old woman asked them into the house. She gave them food to eat and a bed to sleep in.
The children thought she was kind.
She was really a witch. She had made the gingerbread house to trap children. She ate children for dinner.

The witch shut Hansel in a stable.
It had bars in the door.
Then the witch woke Gretel.
"Cook something for your brother,"
she said. "I want to fatten him
up before I eat him."
Gretel wept, but she had to do as
she was told.

Hansel was given the best food.
Gretel was given the scraps. Every
day the witch made Hansel put his
finger through the bars. Every day
Hansel held out a bone instead of
his finger. The witch could not see
very well. Every day she said,
"Not fat enough yet!"

One day the witch could wait
no longer.

"Fetch some water, girl. Fill the
pot!" she said. When that was done,
she said, "Crawl into the oven, girl.
Make sure it is hot." The witch was
going to push Gretel into the oven.

Gretel guessed
what the witch was
going to do.
"I do not know how
to get into the
oven," she said.
"Silly girl!" said
the witch. "I will
show you."
Gretel stood
behind the witch.
She pushed the
witch into the oven.
She closed the door.

It only took a moment to free
Hansel. They filled their pockets
with treasure from the witch's house.
Then they set off to find their way
home. A white duck took them part
of the way.

At last they came to a part of
the forest they knew. Soon they saw
their own house.

The woodcutter was very glad to see
them. He told them their stepmother
was dead.

They sold the treasure and the three
of them lived happily ever after.

All these appear in the pages of
the story. Can you find them?

woodcutter

Hansel

Gretel

pebbles